Liam Says "Hi"

Learning to Greet a Friend

Jane Whelen Banks

Jessica Kingsley Publishers
London and Philadelphia

First published in 2009
by Jessica Kingsley Publishers
116 Pentonville Road
London N1 9JB, UK
and
400 Market Street, Suite 400
Philadelphia, PA 19106, USA

www.jkp.com

Library of Congress Cataloging in Publication Data
Banks, Jane Whelen.
  Liam says "Hi" : learning to greet a friend / Jane Whelen Banks.
    p. cm.
  ISBN 978-1-84310-901-3 (pb : alk. paper)
 1. Self-confidence--Juvenile literature. 2. Confidence--Juvenile literature. 3. Salutations--Juvenile literature. 4. Interpersonal relations--Juvenile literature. 5. Conduct of life--Juvenile literature. I. Title.
  BF575.S39B36 2009
  155.4'18--dc22
                              2008017637

British Library Cataloguing in Publication Data
A CIP catalogue record for this book is available from the British Library

ISBN 978 1 84310 901 3

Printed and bound in China by
Reliance Printing Co, Ltd.

Dedication

To Morgon: Whose patience, love and endless
optimism have cleared many a rain cloud.
Thank you for believing.

Introductions can be awkward for many children. For some, however, making eye contact, and acknowledging another person by simply saying "hi" can be a constant challenge. Yet this instantaneous glance and verbal gesture are essential cues to initiating an interaction. Missing or avoiding this seemingly simple first step can leave potential pals disengaged and foil a play date before it begins. **Liam Says "Hi"** provides step-by-step instructions on how a typical preschooler might receive a friend. It illustrates the importance of facial contact, and offers a simple strategy to cope with the intensity felt when eyes meet. In **Liam Says "Hi"**, Liam completes the steps necessary in greeting a friend at the front door. Appropriately welcomed, Liam's buddy enters the house and both children proceed to have an enjoyable play date.

This is Liam.

Liam has lots of friends who love him
and want to play with him.

Sometimes Liam goes to his
friends' house to play.

Sometimes Liam's friends
come to play at his house.

When we get together with friends, we greet them by looking at their face and saying, "Hi."

We don't look down, or look away
and say nothing.

We don't run off when friends arrive.
They will think we don't want to play.

Instead, take a second to look at your friends' face. You may see a smiling, loving face. You can look at their nose when you say "hi." Or you might want to try looking at their eyes.

See if they see you. Look for the love in their eyes and show them the love in yours.

By looking at their face, your friends will know you are feeling well and that you want to play. They will be glad that you have noticed them.

Liam's friends feel welcome when they come to his house.

They feel connected and special because Liam looks at them and says, "hi" when he greets them. They know that Liam is interested in them.

Liam's friends are happy that Liam wants to play.
Liam is a friendly boy and a great buddy.